FOR VIVIEN, ZANTHE, AND ASA—A.M.

FOR MOMS AND KIDS EVERYWHERE.
IT IS A JOURNEY.
FEED WELL.
EAT WELL.
BE WELL.
—C.A.M.

TO MY MOM, WHO ALWAYS MADE ME TRY JUST
ONE BITE, AND NOW I LOVE IT ALL.—M.B.

Dial Books for Young Readers
An imprint of Penguin Random House LLC, New York

First published in the United States of America by Dial Books for Young Readers,
an imprint of Penguin Random House LLC, 2022

Text copyright © 2022 by Camila Alves McConaughey and Adam Mansbach
Illustrations copyright © 2022 by Mike Boldt

Visit us online at penguinrandomhouse.com.

Library of Congress Cataloging-in-Publication Data is available.

Printed in China
ISBN 9780593324141
Special Markets ISBN 9780593624678 Not for resale
10 9 8 7 6 5 4 3 2 1
RRD

Design by Jennifer Kelly
Text handlettered by Mike Boldt
The artwork was created using Adobe Photoshop and Corel Painter.

JUST TRY ONE BITE

written by
ADAM MANSBACH &
CAMILA ALVES
McCONAUGHEY

illustrated by
MIKE BOLDT

DIAL BOOKS FOR YOUNG READERS

Hi Mama. Hi Papa.
It's time we had a chat
about oatmeal and carrots
and pasta and cake.

And mustard and custard
and chicken-fried steak.
About pork butts and peanuts
and the choices we make.

Let's see here, I wrote down
some points on my checklist.
Number one: No more
ice cream sundaes for breakfast.

I know they're quite tasty
but it's kind of reckless,
like wearing a live
rattlesnake as a necklace.

And I thought that you both
would grow out of this phase
of eating, for lunch,
a whole jar of mayonnaise.

Plus a well-balanced dinner
really ought to be more
than some French fries you found
in your car on the floor.

Your body needs vegetables,
green ones and red ones.
You gotta eat lots of them
to be well-fed ones.
And I know that you hate
the way broccoli tastes,
and you prefer chips
mashed up into a paste
and washed down with a glass of industrial waste...

But the best food of all, the food that really rocks,
comes straight off a tree, not straight out of a box.
We call these foods whole foods
or help-you-to-grow foods,
not fast food
but slooow foods.
Help-you-
bounce-back- if-
you're-sick-
like-they-were-
yo-yo foods.

So how about this:
I'll make you a deal.
Can you just try one bite
and see how you feel?

Those barf sounds you're making aren't very mature. Big kids like you can do better, I'm sure.

Please, darlings,
stop covering your mouths with your hands.
I'll give you 'til three to open up,
Understand?
One...
Two...
whew!
Good job!

Hey!
That's for you
to eat!
YOU!
Not the dog!

Oh Papa, oh Mama,
please be open-minded.
You can't say kale's gross
if you won't even try it.
Look, here comes the airplane!
Straight into the hangar.
Stop kicking and screaming!
What's with all the anger?
I'm not saying you'll never eat frosting again.
Just not every day, more like now and then.

How about this:
If you eat all your veggies,
you can skip tonight's bath
and your room can stay messy.

Have 2 spoons of quinoa
and 3 bites of spinach,
and you can stay up
for an extra 12 minutes.

Here we go! Yum!
I told you so!
It's delicious!

Fine. Just forget it.
I gave you a chance.
Keep hiding your peas
in the cuffs of your pants.
I was going to say
we could all watch a movie,
but you, Mom and Dad,
are behaving quite rudely.

So it's straight off to bed,
and no stories tonight.

Or...you could both
try one teeny bite.

I know you think cauliflower's weird and bizarre.

But just give it a taste

and I'll buy you a car.

I'll let you play hooky from work for a week.

Do we have a deal?

Finally!

Open your beak.

Aha! I knew it!

After all of that fussing,
you like it!
You love it!
You fought us
for nothing!

I'm glad we got over
all the hang-ups you had.
Sometimes kids just know best.

In your face, Mom and Dad!

Sorry, sorry,
I got carried away.
Let's try that again.
What I **meant** to say
is I'm so proud of you,
my adventurous eaters.
My celery-crunching,
beet-munching, egg beaters.

Now let's sit down to dinner!
I roasted some yams
and whipped up a dish
of linguini with clams.
And if you eat every
last bite in your bowls,
then maybe I'll give you
a few...

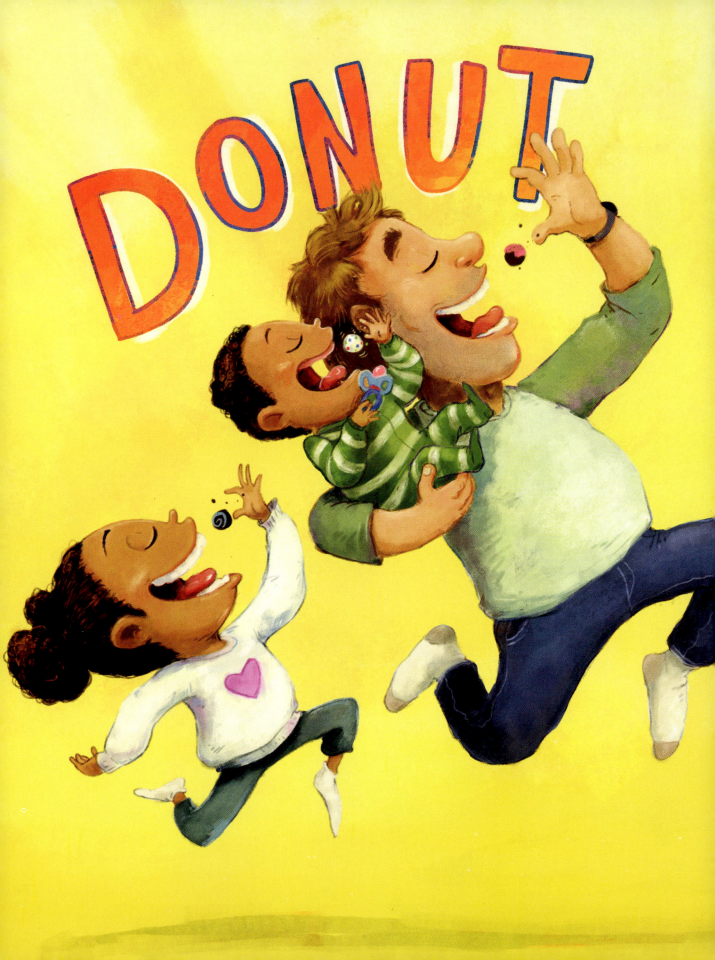